First published in 1995 by Ultimate Editions

© 1995 Anness Publishing Limited

Ultimate Editions is an imprint of
Anness Publishing Limited
Boundary Row Studios
1 Boundary Row
London SE1 8HP

ISBN 1 86035 026 7

Editorial Director Joanna Lorenz
Editorial Consultant Jackie Fortey
Project Editor Belinda Wilkinson

Printed and bound in China

A Storyteller Book

Sleeping Beauty

by Charles Perrault

Retold by Lesley Young
Illustrated by Jenny Press

ULTIMATE
EDITIONS

Many years ago, a king and queen lived in a large and magnificent white castle which had many tall towers and turrets.

The king and queen had almost everything they could wish for, but still they were not happy. The one thing they wished for the most, they could not have and that was a child of their own.

"How I wish we had a prince or princess to play hide and seek with among the apple trees," they sighed in the spring.

"Wouldn't it be lovely to have a child to build a snowman for?" they said in the winter.

One summer day the queen was soaking in her large silver bathtub which was beside an open window. Suddenly a green frog jumped in through the window and landed with a splash in her bath.

"Help!" screamed the queen. But the frog croaked, "Don't be frightened. Before a year is past, a princess will be born who will be as beautiful as I am ugly."

The frog was right. Soon the queen had a princess who was so beautiful that the king cried tears of joy and said,

"She was well worth waiting for."

The king decided to give a huge feast for all his family and friends, to celebrate the baby's birth.

"Don't forget to invite the fairies," said the queen. "You know that they can bring magic gifts, and they will bless our princess with luck and happiness."

There were thirteen fairies in the kingdom, but the king only had twelve gold plates. Everyone knew that fairies only ate off golden plates, so he only sent out twelve invitations. The thirteenth fairy was old and stooped, and the king thought she would be glad to rest at home.

"We will send her some cake after the feast," he said.

The day of the party came, and the palace cooks prepared a wonderful feast with heaps and heaps of chickens and hams and mountains of roast potatoes. The pastrychef baked a huge cake with pink icing.

After everyone had eaten, the fairies went up, one by one, to the princess's cradle to give her their presents.

"I give her the gift of laughter," said one, "so that she will never be sad for long."

"I give her the gift of a lovely voice," said another, "so that when she speaks, it will sound like music."

"I give her the gift of goodness," said a sensible-looking fairy, "so that she will not be loved for her beauty alone."

Eleven fairies had given their presents, and the king and queen were glowing with pride, when suddenly the doors of the banquet hall flew open and everyone gasped.

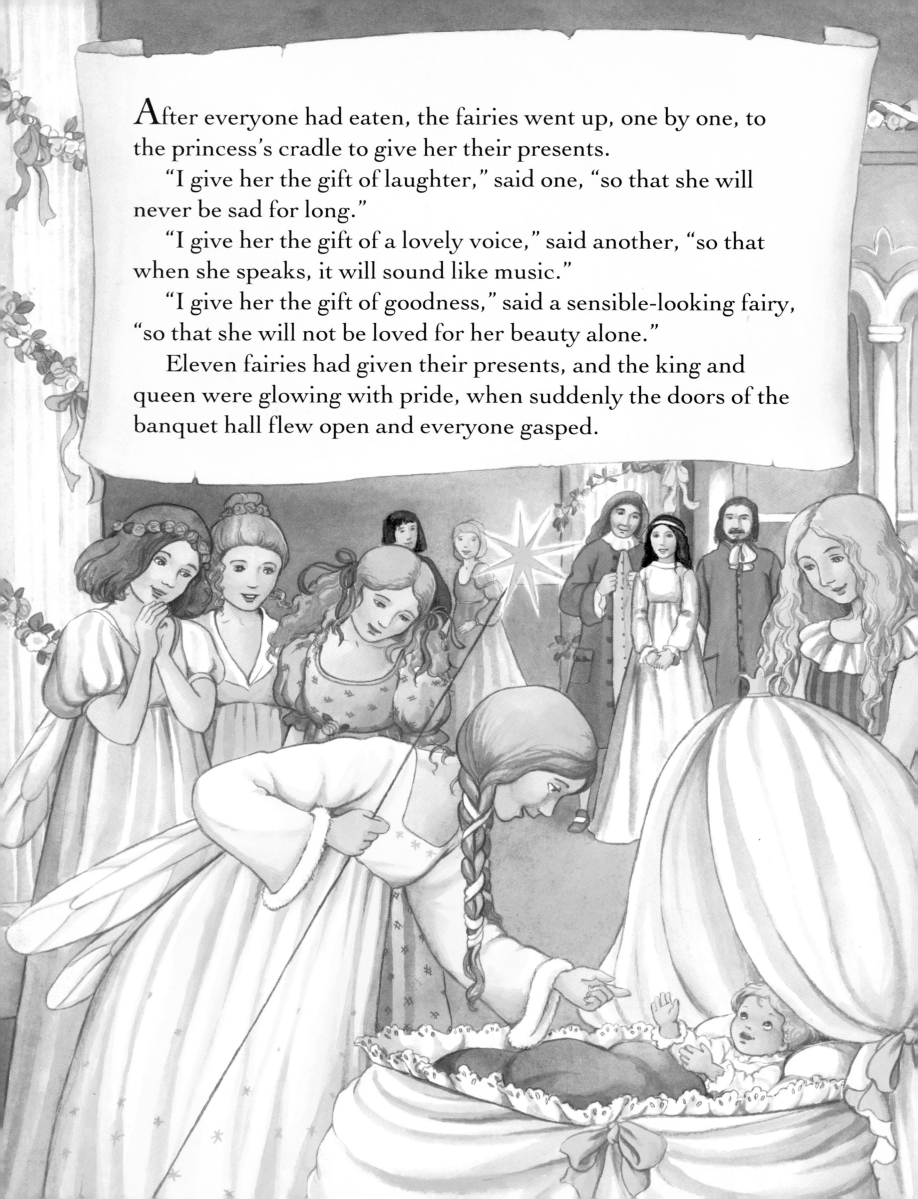

Suddenly, into the room hobbled the oldest fairy, dressed in a black cloak, and shuffling along with the help of a cane.

"So you didn't bother to ask me?" she cackled bitterly, "Well, I came anyway. And of course I too have brought the princess a magic gift."

Then, the oldest fairy hobbled over to the cradle and pointed a long bony finger down at the baby.

"When you are sixteen," she cursed, "you will prick your finger on a spindle and fall down dead!"

Then she turned, and before anyone could speak, she was gone from the room.

All the guests were speechless with shock, and the queen burst into tears.

Everyone had forgotten the twelfth fairy. She had not yet made her gift, and now she stepped forward.

"I can't wipe out another fairy's magic spell," she said, and the queen sobbed more loudly, "but I can help a little. The princess will prick her finger on a spindle, but instead of dying, she will fall into a deep sleep that will last for a hundred years."

The king did everything he could to try and escape the curse on his beloved daughter. He made a law that all spindles were banned from his kingdom, and they were all gathered up and thrown on a huge bonfire.

Posters were stuck everywhere warning that anyone found with a spindle would spend the rest of their days locked in the deepest dungeon in the king's castle.

The princess grew up to be beautiful, happy and good, and the king and queen tried to forget about the terrible curse.

On the princess's sixteenth birthday, everyone was busy preparing for her party.

She looked into the ballroom, and the maids screeched, "Go away! We're decorating the walls!"

She went into the greenhouse and the gardeners shouted, "Go away, the flowers are supposed to be a surprise!"

The princess loved running down to the kitchen for a slice of bread warm from the oven, with honey. The servants were always glad to see her, because she was kind to everyone, but today they said,

"Go away! For heaven's sake, you might have seen your birthday cake!"

Everywhere the princess went, people said, "Go away. It's a surprise!"

The king and queen had driven off in their
carriage to fetch a small, golden puppy they
were going to give her. At last, the princess
was so bored, that she decided to explore
some parts of the castle where she had
never been.

She looked in dusty rooms and along
hallways with creaky floorboards. Suddenly
she came to a narrow, winding staircase that
she had never seen before.

"I wonder where that leads," she
thought. She climbed the stairs, and
cobwebs brushed against her golden hair.

At the top of the stairs was a thick, wooden door, and from behind it came singing and a strange, whirring noise.

The princess pushed open the door and went in. A little old woman was sitting at a spinning wheel, singing and holding something pink and fluffy. Her spindle moved as fast as the wind, its point catching the light from the window.

"What are you doing?" asked the princess.

"I'm spinning some fine pink silk," said the woman.

"Oh, how clever!" said the princess, watching the spindle going back and forwards. "What a clever machine. Can I try?"

She reached out her hand. As soon as she touched the spindle, she pricked her finger and fell down on to the pile of silk, in a deep, deep sleep.

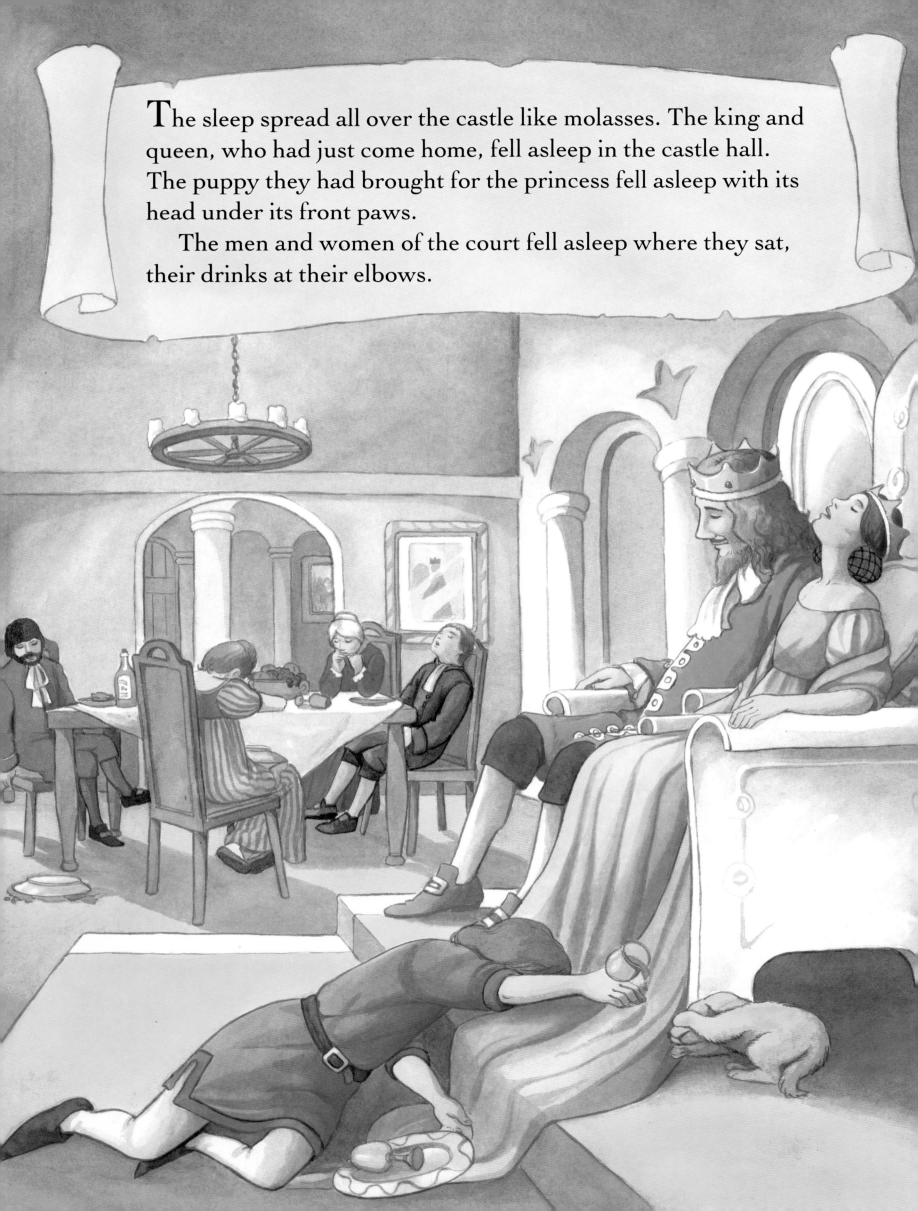

The sleep spread all over the castle like molasses. The king and queen, who had just come home, fell asleep in the castle hall. The puppy they had brought for the princess fell asleep with its head under its front paws.

The men and women of the court fell asleep where they sat, their drinks at their elbows.

The horses in the stables fell asleep standing up and all the grooms and stable boys sank down onto bales of hay and slept where they fell. The pigeons on the roof fell asleep, and so did the flies on the walls and the spiders in the corners.

All the fires that had been blazing in the fireplaces died down and the meat stopped sizzling on its spit. The cook, who was just about to scold the kitchen boy sank into sleep, just missing a vat of gravy.

The wind dropped, and the flags on the turrets stopped fluttering. It was as if the whole castle held its breath.

A thick hedge of sharp thorns began to grow all around the castle walls.

Every year it grew some more, until the whole castle was hidden, even to the tip of its highest flag pole.

Many years passed and stories grew up about what lay behind the hedge of thorns.

"When I was very small, my mother told me that there was a castle with a beautiful princess fast asleep behind there," said a very old man.

But others thought that a witch or a monster lived there and warned their children not to go near.

One bright morning, a handsome young prince came riding into the kingdom.

"Where is the magic castle with the beautiful princess?" he asked. "My grandfather has told me all about her, and I am here to rescue her."

Everyone laughed at him. "We have heard that story, too," they said. "There have been other princes who have come here. They have tried to cut their way through the hedge, but they have all been trapped in the thorns and left to die."

One of the good fairies heard that the prince had arrived in the kingdom, and was asking everyone where the castle was.

She was very worried, because the hundred years would not be over until the next day. She knew that if the prince tried to cut his way through the hedge he, too, would be trapped in the sharp thorns.

So, the good fairy thought of a plan that would slow down the prince's journey, and also let her know if he was as good as he was handsome.

The prince was riding along a road when he came upon an old man trying to cut down a tree. He was huffing and puffing and could hardly swing his axe.

The prince got off his horse and tied it to a tree.

"Can I be of help, old man?" he called, striding over.

"My fire has gone out and I am too old and weak to cut any wood," said the old man, who was really the fairy in disguise.

"Stand aside!" said the prince, and he took the axe and cut down the tree. Then he chopped it into firewood and stacked it outside the old man's cottage.

"Thank you," said the old man. "Good luck will follow your kindness."

"I hope so," said the prince. "I am looking for the castle with the sleeping princess," and he rode on his way.

Next, the fairy turned herself into a cat and jumped down to the bottom of an empty well.

The prince was riding along, when he suddenly felt so tired that he got off his horse and sat down to rest beside the well. He took some bread and cheese out of his saddlebag, and had just begun to eat when he heard a faint, mewing noise. He looked all around but could see nothing.

At last he traced the sound to the old well. Looking over the rim, he saw a black and white cat, looking very sorry for itself, at the bottom of the well.

"If I leave it there, it will surely starve to death," he said.

The prince looked around for some rope, but could see none.

In the field beside him, there grew some long, tough grass. The prince cut a good bunch with his sword, and braided them into a rope. Then he tied the rope to the end of his horse's tail and backed the horse up to the edge of the well. He dropped the rope down until it reached the bottom and called down,

"Grab onto the grass with your claws, little cat, and hold on tight. We'll soon have you out."

The cat gripped the grass rope, the prince led the horse forward from the well, and the cat was pulled up.

"There we are," he said, setting it free.

The cat purred, and the prince could almost have sworn that it said, "Good luck."

The prince rode on. There was still no sign of the hedge of
thorns, and he could see no one to ask. Suddenly, in front of him
on the road, he saw an old woman, struggling with a huge and
heavy bundle.

"Can I help you?" called down the prince from his horse.

"I have to get my bundle home before nightfall," said the old
woman, "but it seems to be growing heavier at every step."

"Do you live near here?" asked the prince.

"I live at the very end of that path, in the middle of nowhere,"
she said, pointing down the dusty lane.

It was surely out of the prince's way, but he said, "Come up
behind me on my good horse, and I will speed you home."

He reached down and helped her up. Then he hoisted the
bundle up in front of him and set forth, and at every stride the
horse took, the weight of the old woman and the bundle seemed
to grow lighter and lighter. At last they reached her old,
rundown cottage, just as night was falling.

"I am looking for the hedge of thorns, and the castle with the beautiful, sleeping princess," explained the prince as he helped the old woman dismount from his horse.

"Stay here tonight," said the old woman. "You can't travel in the dark. I'm afraid I can only give you a mattress on the floor and some stew."

The prince was not proud, and stayed the night. He was surprised to find that the stew was the best food he had ever tasted, and the mattress felt as soft as a feather bed.

In the morning, the old woman, who was, of course, the fairy, thanked him.

"Turn right at the end of the path," she told him. "Good luck will follow your kindness."

The prince did as she said, and there, right in front of him, rose the thick hedge of thorns.

"How strange," he thought. "I'm sure I would have noticed this yesterday."

At that very moment, the hundred years had just finished. He rode on his horse to the hedge of thorns and as he trotted up, it burst into blossom before his very eyes. A path opened up in the hedge and he was able to ride through, the blossom waving all around him. At last he had found the castle.

The prince got off his horse and marched up to the castle. In the yard, he saw horses sleeping standing up and cats curled up like fat, soft cushions. In the hall he found the king and queen, fast asleep on the floor beside the puppy. He explored some more and found all the men and women of the court slumped in their chairs, fast asleep.

He clattered, in his silver spurs, down to the kitchens. There was the cook fast asleep with her mouth open and the kitchen boy sleeping with a worried look on his face.

A kitchen maid was sitting, sound asleep, holding a chicken that was half plucked.

The prince looked in all the bedrooms but, of course, they were empty because it was morning when the sleep had crept over the entire castle.

"I will search every corner until I find the princess!" he said, and his voice echoed from the silent, stone walls – the first sound in a hundred years.

At last the prince found the winding staircase that led to the highest turret. He climbed it and pushed open the creaky, heavy door. Inside lay the princess, as beautiful as ever, with a slight smile on her lips as if she were dreaming. The prince, who had never seen anything as lovely, did not stop to think. He kneeled down beside her and kissed her gently.

At the touch of his lips, the princess woke up, stretched her arms above her head, and smiled at him.

"I've had such a lovely long sleep," she said, "I wouldn't be surprised if it was nearly dinner time. Shall we go and see?"

The prince and princess went downstairs hand in hand, and found the king and queen waking up. The puppy woke up and began to bark. The people at court woke up and finished their drinks. The cook woke up and scolded the kitchen boy. The fire leapt up again and the meat turned on its spit. The kitchen maid woke up and continued plucking the chicken.

Out in the yard the horses woke up and shook their manes. The grooms woke up and the cats woke and stretched. The flies crawled up the walls and the spiders scurried in corners.

The princess led the prince down to meet her parents.

"Happy birthday!" they said to her.

The princess held out the prince's hand. "I have had the loveliest dream," she said, "and look at the wonderful birthday present I woke up to find!"

The castle door opened, and there stood the old woman the prince had helped the day before.

"What are you doing here?" he asked.

At that moment, the old woman changed back into the good fairy and said,

"The hundred years are up. The spell is broken!"

The king and queen gasped with joy and when the prince asked if he could marry their daughter, they agreed at once.

"Instead of a birthday party, we will have a wedding!" they said happily.

As word spread throughout the castle that the spell was broken,
everyone began to dance wildly with one another and cheer.
But the prince looked into the princess's lovely eyes and
said joyfully,
"For us, the magic is only just beginning."